Busy Little Mouse

For Robyn, who keeps me connected — E.F.
For Mom, the busiest mouse I know — K.F.

Text © 2002 Eugenie Fernandes
Illustrations © 2002 Kim Fernandes

Photography by Pat Lacroix

Kids Can Press acknowledges the financial support of the Ontario Arts Council, the Canada Council
for the Arts and the Government of Canada, through the BPIDP, for our publishing activity.

Published in Canada by
Kids Can Press Ltd.
29 Birch Avenue
Toronto, ON M4V 1E2

Published in the U.S. by
Kids Can Press Ltd.
2250 Military Road
Tonawanda, NY 14150

www.kidscanpress.com

The artwork in this book was rendered in Fimo®, a pliable modeling material.
Text is set in Avenir.

Edited by Debbie Rogosin
Designed by Julia Naimska
Printed in Hong Kong, China, by Wing King Tong Company Limited

This book is smyth sewn casebound.

CM 02 0 9 8 7 6 5 4 3 2

National Library of Canada Cataloguing in Publication Data

Fernandes, Eugenie, 1943–
Busy little mouse

ISBN 1-55074-776-2

I. Fernandes, Kim II. Title.

PS8561.E7596B88 2002   jC813'.54   C2001-901515-1
PZ7.F3624Bu 2002

Kids Can Press is a *Corus*™ Entertainment company

Busy Little Mouse

Written by **Eugenie Fernandes**

Illustrated by **Kim Fernandes**

KIDS CAN PRESS

Busy Little Mouse
hurries out to play
and bumps into a bouncy dog.
What does the little dog say?

**Woof!
Woof!**

The bouncy little dog
wants to play all day
in puddles with a wiggly pig.
What does the little pig say?

Oink!
Oink!

The wiggly little pig,
in a playful sort of way,
hugs and tugs a timid sheep.
What does the little sheep say?

Baa!
Baa!

The timid little sheep
tries to hide away
underneath a friendly cow.
What does the little cow say?

Moo!
Moo!

The friendly little cow,
nibbling some hay,
stops and licks a happy cat.
What does the little cat say?

Meow!
Meow!

The happy little cat
goes scampering away,
racing with a noisy duck.
What does the little duck say?

Quack!
Quack!

The noisy little duck
splashes in the bay,
startling a gentle horse.
What does the little horse say?

**Neigh!
Neigh!**

The gentle little horse,
smooth and silver gray,
gallops around with Little Mouse.
What does Little Mouse say?

Squeak!
Squeak!

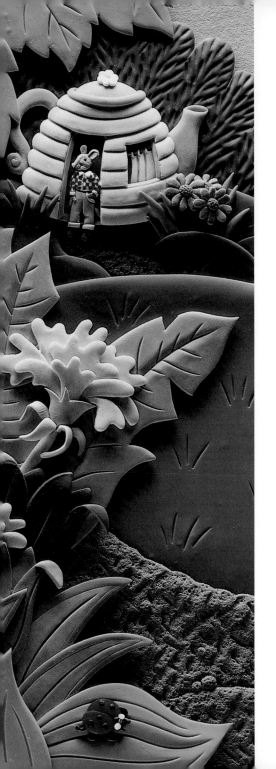

Weary Little Mouse —
what a busy day!
Running, bumping,
splashing, jumping,
scampering away.

Hurry home.
Climb into bed.
Read a book.
Rest your head.

Blow a kiss.
Turn out the light.
We love you, Little Mouse …

Good night.